THE TOY CIRCUS

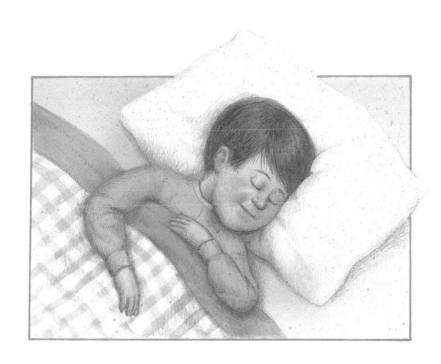

For Aase and Poul Malmkjaer
—Jan Wahl

For Keryn, Brynne and Megan
—Tim Bowers

Requests for permission to make copies of any
part of the work should be mailed to:
Permissions Department, Harcourt Brace Jovanovich, Publishers,
8th Floor, Orlando, Florida 32887.

Jacket and book design by Art Direction, Inc.

Library of Congress Cataloging-in-Publication Data
Wahl, Jan.
The toy circus,
"Gulliver books."
Summary: From a quiet box in a young child's room
erupts a nighttime circus with the dreaming child
self-cast as ringmaster.
[1. Circus—Fiction.   2. Dreams—Fiction.
3. Stories in rhyme]   I. Bowers, Tim, ill.   II. Title.
PZ8.3.W133To   1986   [E]   85-30186
ISBN 0-15-200609-5

Printed in the United States of America
B C D E F

THE TOY CIRCUS

WRITTEN BY JAN WAHL

ILLUSTRATED BY TIM BOWERS

GULLIVER BOOKS
HARCOURT BRACE JOVANOVICH

SAN DIEGO   NEW YORK   LONDON

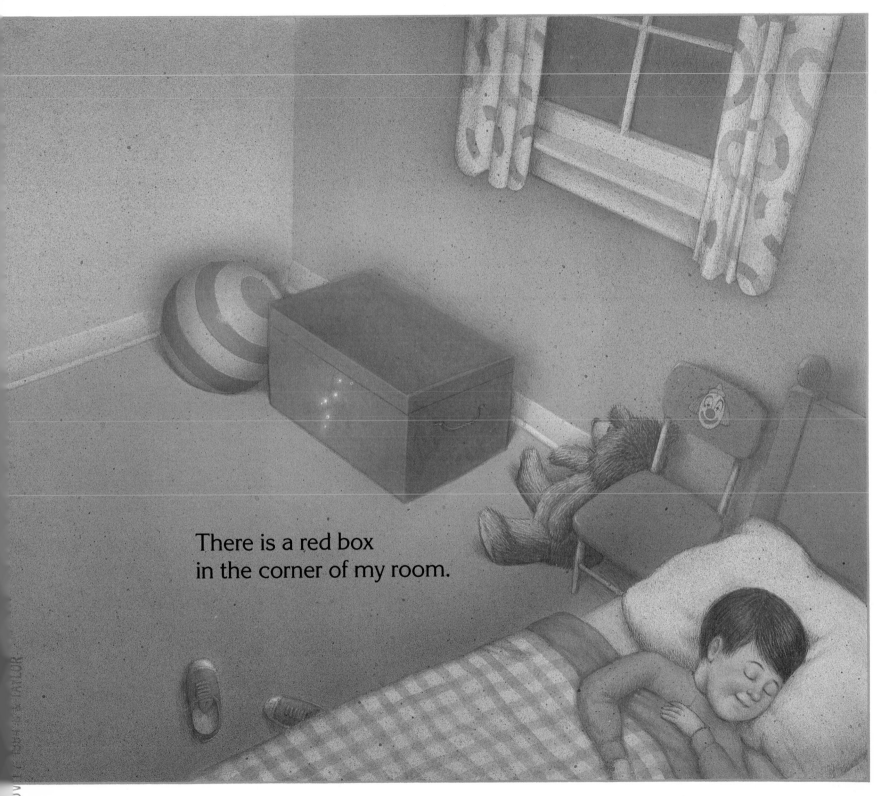

There is a red box
in the corner of my room.

Each night
a little clown
peeks out,

and soon...

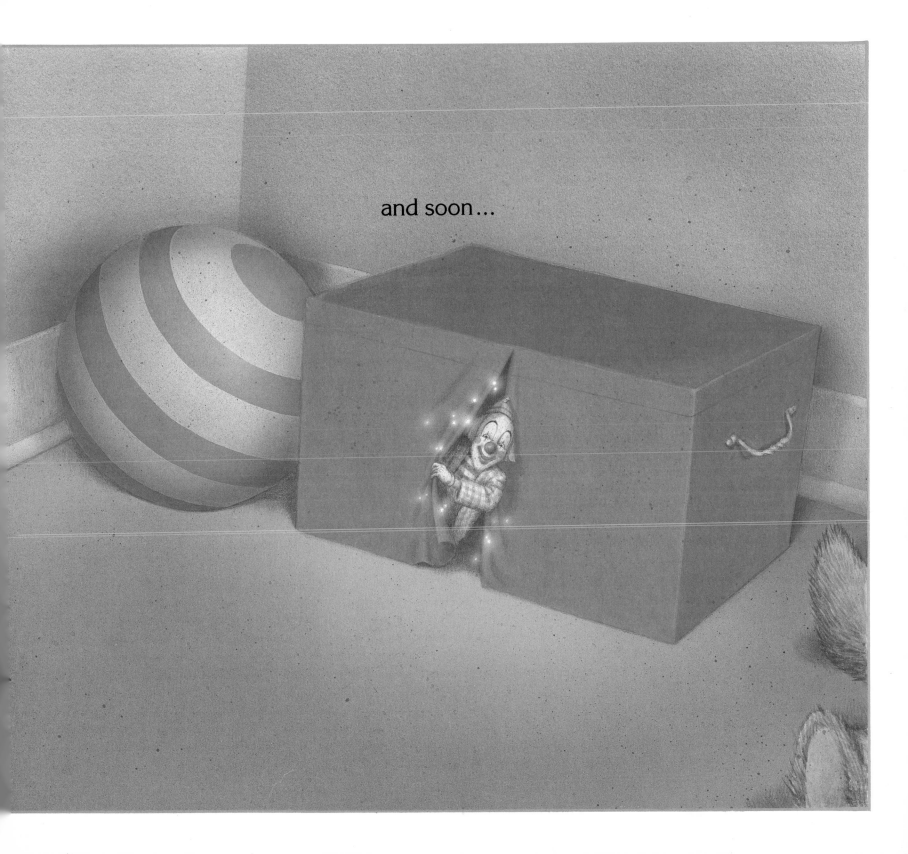

A plump lady follows
on one foot, hup.
Another is riding
downside up.

Brown bears roll by
in a gilded cart.

Tiger comes running
with another clown drumming.
Rum pum pum,
pum pum pum.

I am the ringmaster.
I snap my whip.

Loud calliope
fills the room
with a merry din.

Oom pah pah
Oom pah.
Let the circus begin!

Plumed ponies prance,
plump ladies dance.

Rum pum pum pum.
Oom pah pah.

Rum pum pum, oh
here walks clown.

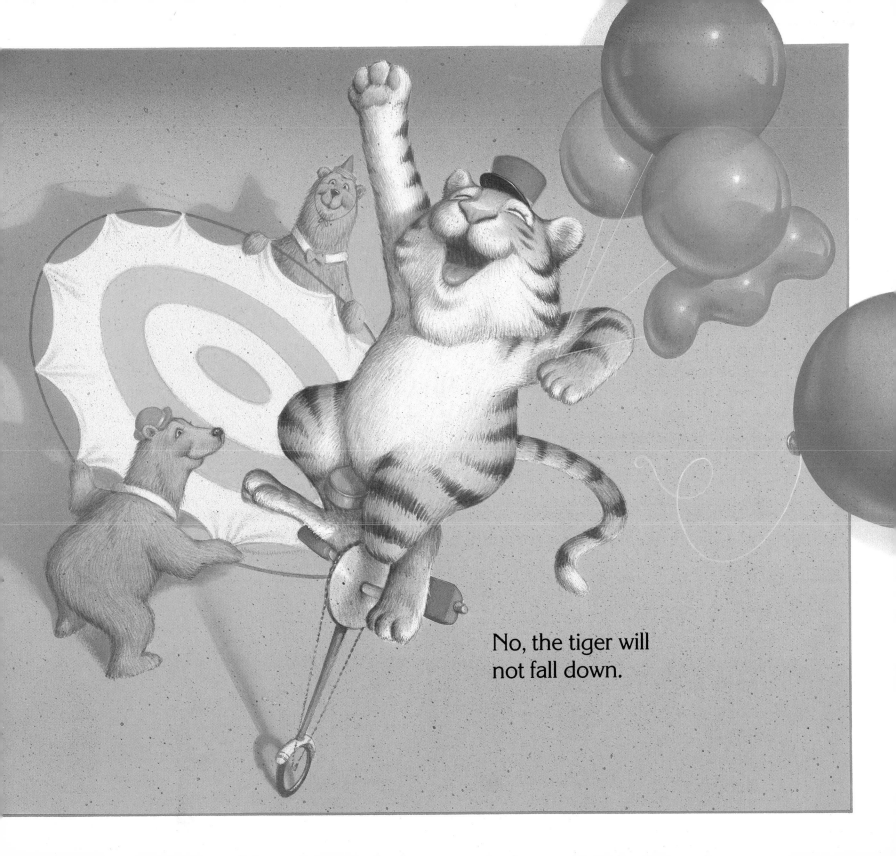

No, the tiger will
not fall down.

Lots of bright parasols
wheel around my ring.

Bears climb high —
balance and swing.

Rum pum pum,
whoops, one bear
stumbles.

Tiger helps him
while two clowns
tumble.

Rockets burst
at the cannon's boom.
Clown flies up with
a loud ka-foom!

Two plump ladies and
quick tiger jump—
land on ponies without a bump.

But
dreaming toys
must end
their nighttime ride.

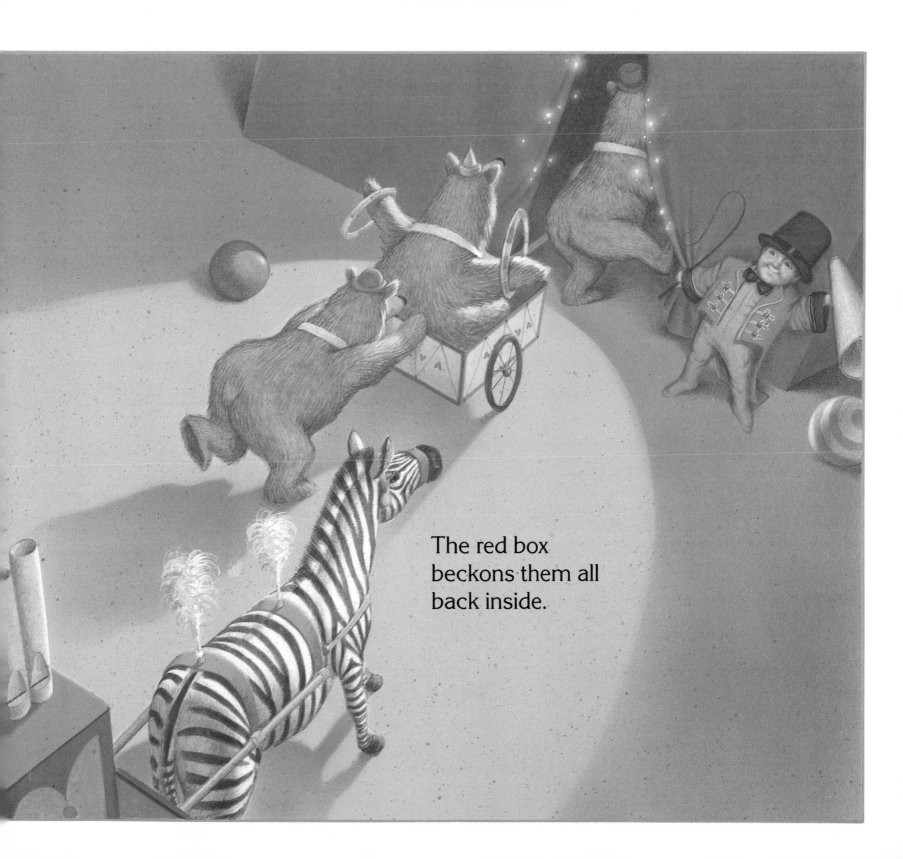

The red box
beckons them all
back inside.

Sizzling sparklers
shed one last brilliant light.

Fa la beetle
boom boom.

Little clown
sweeps the dust,

shuts the flaps,

Good night!